Acting Edition

Eternal Life
Part 1

by Nathan Alan Davis

SAMUEL FRENCH

FOR PRODUCTION INQUIRIES

UNITED STATES AND CANADA
info@concordtheatricals.com
1-866-979-0447

UNITED KINGDOM AND EUROPE
licensing@concordtheatricals.co.uk
020-7054-7298

Each title is subject to availability from Concord Theatricals Corp., depending upon country of performance. Please be aware that *ETERNAL LIFE PART 1* may not be licensed by Concord Theatricals Corp. in your territory. Professional and amateur producers should contact the nearest Concord Theatricals Corp. office or licensing partner to verify availability.

No one shall make any changes in this title(s) for the purpose of production. No part of this book may be reproduced, stored in a retrieval system, scanned, uploaded, or transmitted in any form, by any means, now known or yet to be invented, including mechanical, electronic, digital, photocopying, recording, videotaping, or otherwise, without the prior written permission of the publisher. No one shall share this title(s), or any part of this title(s), through any social media or file hosting websites.

For all inquiries regarding motion picture, television, online/digital and other media rights, please contact Concord Theatricals Corp.

MUSIC AND THIRD-PARTY MATERIALS USE NOTE

Licensees are solely responsible for obtaining formal written permission from copyright owners to use copyrighted music and/or other copyrighted third-party materials (e.g. artworks, logos) in the performance of this play and are strongly cautioned to do so. If no such permission is obtained by the licensee, then the licensee must use only original music and materials that the licensee owns and controls. Licensees are solely responsible and liable for clearances of all third-party copyrighted materials, including without limitation music, and shall indemnify the copyright owners of the play(s) and their licensing agent, Concord Theatricals Corp., against any costs, expenses, losses and liabilities arising from the use of such copyrighted third-party materials by licensees. For music, please contact the appropriate music licensing authority in your territory for the rights to any incidental music.

IMPORTANT BILLING AND CREDIT REQUIREMENTS

If you have obtained performance rights to this title, please refer to your licensing agreement for important billing and credit requirements.

ETERNAL LIFE PART 1 was originally commissioned and produced by the Wilma Theater, Philadelphia, PA, on April 11, 2023. The performance was directed by Morgan Green, with sets by Matt Saunders, costumes by Azalea Fairley, lighting by Masha Tsimring, sound design by Jordan McCree, and projection design by Alan Price. The production stage manager was Patreshettarlini Adams and the assistant stage manager was Chloe Kincade. The cast was as follows:

WOMAN / MOTHER SNOWFLAKE................Jennifer Kidwell
JUNIOR / SNOWFLAKE CHILD /
HEARSE DRIVER ....Brandon J. Pierce
GRAY-BEARDED MAN / DEATH CONSULTANT .....Lindsay Smiling
GOOSE ....Sarah Gliko
MAN / FATHER SNOWFLAKE ....Steven Rishard
VOICE ....Pax Ressler

CHARACTERS

WOMAN
MOTHER SNOWFLAKE

MAN
FATHER SNOWFLAKE

GOOSE

SNOWFLAKE CHILD
JUNIOR
HEARSE DRIVER

GRAY-BEARDED MAN
DEATH CONSULTANT

AUTHOR'S NOTES

An ellipsis on its own line

...

represents a pause, a beat, or perhaps a physical action.

A slash / marks the beginning of an overlap.

SPECIAL THANKS

Morgan Green for championing this play and bringing it to such powerful life at the Wilma.

The Wilma's HotHouse Ensemble and Jennifer Kidwell for your collaboration and artistry.

Ben Pesner, Peter Richards, and Venturous Theater Fund for supporting the world premiere.

Seonjae Kim and Mandy Greenfield for early conversations that helped me identify the essence of the story.

Andrea Hiebler and Krista Williams for your galvanizing encouragement long before this script took its present form.

ACT ONE

One

(Night. **WOMAN** *and* **MAN** *are in their most recently acquired home.)*

(There is a very large window. It is snowing outside.)

*(***WOMAN*** *looks out the window. She takes a long sip from a cup of tea. She's trying her best to enjoy the moment.)*

(But something catches her attention.)

(It's a **GOOSE**, *which is outside in the yard.)*

WOMAN. The goose is staring at us.

MAN. *Staring?* I'm not sure if that's...um –

WOMAN. What would you call that?

MAN. Well.

We're new here.

So I'd call it curiosity.

WOMAN. I don't remember a goose being discussed. As part of the purchase.

MAN. It was discussed.

It was a perk.

WOMAN. Okay but she's staring directly at me.

MAN. If you're not happy with the place, let's talk about that. Let's not make it about the goose.

WOMAN. ...

MAN. We can sell, you know.

WOMAN. We *just* moved in.

MAN. Exactly. So, if it's not working...now would be the perfect time to cut bait. Minimal furniture? Seller's market?

WOMAN. ...

MAN. I mean how long do you think we really need to give it?

WOMAN. More than a *day*.

MAN. Okay, so...how long?

WOMAN. Six months? A year? I mean...to give it a fair shot.

MAN. What can you learn in a year that you can't learn in a day?

WOMAN. Is that a serious question?

MAN. ...

I think the problem, actually, is that you haven't quite...

Don't take this the wrong way:

WOMAN. Okay, I'm gonna need you to pause. And think about what you're about to say / before you –

MAN. Right, yeah, good idea.

(**WOMAN** *finishes her tea.*)

WOMAN. Would you like some water? I really like the tap water here, don't you?

MAN. No, thanks.

WOMAN. …

MAN. I'm good for now.

> (**WOMAN** *exits.*)

> (**MAN** *gets up. Paces for a bit. Looks out the window.*)

> (*Looks around the mostly empty house.*)

Weather report.

> (*Instantaneously, the walls of the house light up with information. Stock prices. Graphs describing air quality and water purity. Movie trailers. Several ads for furniture sales. A voice speaks.*)

VOICE. Good evening!

Looks like you could use help furnishing your place. I'll show you some options while I look up the weather.

> (*Icons of chairs, tables, and sofas are highlighted on the walls, with designations listed below them, such as "only two left" and "free delivery."*)

MAN. Just the weather, please.

VOICE. Of course.

> (*The walls go mostly dark, but a faint glow remains. A temperature reading appears on a wall, along with a moving image of snow falling from a cloud.*)

The current temperature is 24.8 degrees Fahrenheit, negative 4 degrees Celsius. It's snowing like the Dickens out there. Flurries are expected to continue through the night and into tomorrow morning. Here are some options for professional snow removal in the area –

MAN. No thanks.

> (*A calendar appears, listing the weather forecast for the next several days.*)

VOICE. Skies are expected to clear tomorrow afternoon. Here's what the rest of the week looks like.

Also, I went ahead and curated a list of songs, films, and television episodes that you might enjoy on a night like this, cuddled up next to your wife under a blanket as the snow falls outside. Would you like to see it?

MAN. Maybe later.

VOICE. You seem upset. Something on your mind?

MAN. ...

What are the chances of a brain-eating amoeba entering our bodies through the tap water?

VOICE. Roughly one in 200 billion.

MAN. So. Not zero.

VOICE. Perhaps a comparison would help. In your present environment, you are about as likely to be killed by a meteorite crashing through your window as you are to be killed by a brain-eating amoeba.

> (**MAN** *looks out the window. And up into the sky.*)

This conversation doesn't seem to be helping. Enjoy the evening!

> (*The walls return to normal again.*)

> (**MAN** *sits back in his chair. Looks out the window.*)

> (**WOMAN** *returns with a glass of water.*)

WOMAN. I don't want to install a water filter. Whatever is in the aquifer, I want it. I want all of it. I hope that's okay with you.

MAN. …

Want to watch a movie?

WOMAN. I thought you were going to educate me on "what the problem actually is."

(**WOMAN** *takes a drink of water.*)

Something I haven't quite figured out yet?

MAN. Can we, maybe, reset?

WOMAN. By all means.

MAN. Alright. Let me start with myself.

I'm not entirely comfortable. With the way the water tastes.

That doesn't mean I can't get used to it.

But, at the same time,

Why should I have to?

You know? Just like, for you, if there's anything about any of this that you don't like,

Why should *you* have to?

WOMAN. Have to what? Have problems?

MAN. Growing up like I grew up.

Where you just kind of…*have* things.

There's a certain discipline to it, okay?

WOMAN. Go on.

MAN. I learned, kind of by osmosis I guess, that you have to make quick decisions. Because if you don't, just, the sheer number of options alone, the variables, they can get to you.

WOMAN. I can see that.

MAN. So, yeah!

That's all I'm trying to say.

It would be one thing if we *had* to make it work out here. But we *don't*.

We've got the house in Maine.

We've got the Brazil house.

We've got the Hong Kong place.

I think it's quite clear.

I think the proverbial writing is on the proverbial wall.

We thought we might be happier here but we're not, so great, we tried it, let's move on.

WOMAN. On to what?

MAN. Vacation?

We could do one of those low-orbit cruises, maybe?

> *(The walls of the house wake up again. A "raised hand icon" appears on the wall.)*

Go ahead.

VOICE. There is an L.E.O. cruise departing in eight days from Palm Bay, Florida, with four seats available, at present, in the V.I.P. section only. Would you like to make a partially refundable deposit tonight to reserve your tickets?

WOMAN. No, thank you.

VOICE. Should you change your minds, I might suggest a weeklong stay in Miami prior to your launch. I've drawn up a preliminary itinerary. If you'd like to see it, just say the word.

> *(The walls of the house go to sleep again.)*

MAN. You sure? It's just like a regular cruise except it's in space.

WOMAN. Yeah, I know exactly what it is and it sounds terrifying.

MAN. …

You know, when we got married, I thought you were adventurous.

WOMAN. …

MAN. People change.

Or our perception of them changes.

Or both!

That's an observation, not a criticism.

WOMAN. Well. Given that observation.

If I'm not what you thought you were getting in a life partner, I guess you should *move on*. To a person that's more immediately compatible.

MAN. That's not at all what I meant –

WOMAN. That seems to be your life philosophy now –

MAN. It's not my life philosophy. It's a strategy for managing abundance.

WOMAN. What *is* your life philosophy?

MAN. …

Live and let live?

WOMAN. …

MAN. What's *your* life philosophy?

WOMAN. Leave every place you've been better than it was when you found it.

MAN. Oh.

That's. That's really good.

WOMAN. Thank you.

MAN. You actually *do* that, too. That's amazing.

WOMAN. I know I do.

Every day of my life.

MAN. Is that why you want to see this through?

So you can perform your duty, as it were, to this place?

WOMAN. That's part of it. Yes.

I'm sick of not being *rooted*.

I'm sick of not having a place that I can love and hate and for better or worse, it's home.

I'm sick of everything being like...shopping.

I like the fact that there's *work* to do here.

> *(The **WOMAN** looks out the window again.)*

> *(The **GOOSE** has stopped staring but is still present.)*

MAN. Do you want me to kill it?

WOMAN. Oh my God, no, what is wrong with you?

MAN. I mean, if we try to sell her or remove her it would just be a big hassle.

For all we know she'd just, migrate right back.

WOMAN. That is the most repulsive thing I've ever heard you say.

You'd honestly go outside and kill that goose?

MAN. I'd call someone to take care of it.

Humanely.

WOMAN. You'd call a hit on our pet!?

MAN. Okay, it's not a *hit,* and she's not our pet / she just –

WOMAN. She was here before us. We have an obligation to take care of her –

MAN. You said just this morning that you wished she'd drop dead!

WOMAN. I don't want to get everything I want!

MAN. Why not!?

WOMAN. Because my morality is going to atrophy and then I'll become a myopic, entitled, self-righteous waste of land and air, like all the people in the world I hate most!

MAN. How did you learn to express yourself so precisely when you're angry?!

WOMAN. I HAD TO BECAUSE I'M MARRIED TO *YOU*!

(A short silence.)

MAN. Okay, so no space cruise.

We'll work on the house.

We'll uh –

We'll make ourselves useful. Around the neighborhood.

We'll go on walks.

How does that sound?

WOMAN. And I'll start a garden?

A vegetable garden?

MAN. Sure.

WOMAN. And an herb garden.

And a flower garden.

MAN. Of course.

And the goose won't last long.

WOMAN. ...

MAN. I mean,

> It's going to be a temporary problem is what I'm saying.
>
> Because the lifespan of a goose. As compared to the lifespan of a human…there's a gap there.
>
> She'll only be around for ten, fifteen years tops. And then, you know.

> > (**GOOSE** *smiles.*)
>
> > (*And exits.*)

WOMAN. Right.

MAN. And we'll still have four more decades to go.

WOMAN. Sure. Or five or six or seven or eight or nine or ten more decades to go.

MAN. I mean. I'm not interested in living past **eighty**.

WOMAN. Don't say that / what is wrong with you!?

MAN. What? That's what I always say.

WOMAN. …

> I've been thinking, you know?
>
> …
>
> It's so quiet out here.
>
> And this terrible thought
>
> Imposed itself on my mind.

MAN. Yeah?

WOMAN. …

> I really don't want to die.
>
> Like,
>
> Ever.

I want to be immortal.

And not, like, heaven, paradise, immortal-soul-venturing-into-the-vast-unknown. Not that kind of immortal.

I mean like, in the flesh. In this body. With this mind. Me. Never dying.

MAN. ...

Okay.

Um.

Why do you think you want that?

WOMAN. Because.

MAN. Yeah. I mean, / I get it.

WOMAN. Because time will move on, and generations will pass, and all memory, all thought of me in the world will be gone.

Unless I find a way to, you know,

Stay.

MAN. Makes sense.

WOMAN. But that's not really...like...

Possible.

MAN. ...

WOMAN. Think of all the amazing things that are going to happen. A thousand years from now. Ten thousand years from now. A hundred thousand years from now. And we're going to miss *all* of it.

MAN. Do you want to have a baby?

WOMAN. ...

MAN. Our child would be a version of us that gets to see a little farther into the future.

That's

Probably the best we can do.

WOMAN. Wait.

Do *you* want to have a baby?

MAN. I mean, I guess.

WOMAN. Okay, so then *say that.*

MAN. I just did.

WOMAN. "*Fine* if you're so so sad and you wish you were immortal, I guess we can have this baby."

MAN. I did not say / that –

WOMAN. Yes you pretty much did –

MAN. I did not say that I said / "Do you want to have a baby?"

WOMAN. That's exactly what you *did* say and you know it.

If you want to have a baby then say so.

MAN. I want to have a baby.

WOMAN. Oh?

With who?

MAN. With you.

WOMAN. Hm. Interesting.

I'll consider it.

I have a question, though.

MAN. ...

WOMAN. Would you *really* be okay not selling.

And staying here.

Making this a real home. Not just a seasonal place to, like, retreat to.

MAN. Yes, I would.

I'd have to become more like you.

WOMAN. Meaning?

MAN. I'll have to be more at peace with the quiet. With watching the snow gather on the trees and so forth. I mean, I try to be that way sometimes, but it doesn't come naturally. Remember our wedding?

WOMAN. Please don't remind me.

MAN. ...

I'm a better man than I was when you found me.

WOMAN. I'm glad you think so.

That makes me happy.

MAN. Do you think this is a good place to raise a child?

WOMAN. Yes, I do.

> *(They kiss.)*

What will it be like?

MAN. The child?

Or our lives as parents of said child?

WOMAN. The child.

MAN. Who knows?

> *(They kiss.)*

WOMAN. And our lives?

MAN. Who knows?

> *(They kiss.)*

WOMAN. Bring the goose a blanket.

MAN. What?

WOMAN. She's out there in the cold, bring her a blanket.

MAN. She's fine.

WOMAN. I'll be distracted.

It's snowing.

It's cold.

>   (**MAN** *gets a blanket and exits.*)

Two

(A funeral home.)

*(The **GOOSE** enters and stands at a lectern.)*

GOOSE. Welcome to the funeral.

Thanks for being here.

Why am I so...annoyed?

...

Not because the Old Man Who Never Thought I Would Outlive Him is dead.

Not because the Old Woman Who Still Looks Young isn't here with me.

That's her business.

I guess I'm a little miffed, you know, because the one I'm expected to honor here today.

Had a life.

A whole, long, predominantly healthy life.

And he just kinda...

Well, he lived. Successfully. For about **eighty** years.

And for fifty of those eighty years, he imposed himself on my world – and there was little to nothing I could do about it.

I did not choose my orbit.

It was given to me.

By happenstance. By the intermingling of instinct and geography,

Which in my more religious moments I have sometimes called "Fate."

None of us are given the power to decide our orbits, you see.

Well, that's not exactly true:

I had a friend named Zachary.

He's gone now.

But again, concerning the Old Man,

This is one of many millions of funerals.

Billions.

Trillions.

Depending on how wide a net you want to cast and in what directions.

So what should I have to say about the inevitable death

Of a single grain of sand

In the limitless desert

Of reality?

Should I say that there was a certain gleam in his eye?

Should I say that he taught me the meaning of something?

Should I say that I'll never forget that time he stepped on my foot

And later we had a laugh

And eventually the swelling went down?

Shouldn't we all have a laugh *now*?

Shouldn't we lighten the mood?

...

Today also just so happens to be my birthday.

Did anyone bring streamers?

Cake?

Hats?

What is it about party hats?

What do they signify?

A very temporary alliance, I suppose.

...

Anyway, to sum up our relationship: I was already living at the farm. He arrived with his wife. I remained at the farm and changed nothing of my daily habits. He did insulate the barn, eventually, and that was nice. Many decades passed. He rarely forgot to feed me, which is, I think, a kind of love, for those of you that subscribe.

...

I have to ask: did any of you even approach the open casket?

...

Maybe if they put it closer to the snacks.

Well.

...

...

A fish walked into a bar:

It was a lungfish, probably.

...

And that's

The whole joke.

...

...

Lungfish are one of the few species of fish that can walk on land.

...

The bar, as luck would have it, must have been right on the shore of a lake, otherwise the lungfish never could have reached it.

So there's the,

The aftershock of the joke as it were.

...

Of course *real* aftershocks are not funny at all.

Which brings us back to our topic.

Death.

...

Death is where all of us mortal beings are headed, no matter what. So: What's the point of all the life that happens along the way?

Perhaps just as importantly, what *is* a point?

And why

Do we have to keep making them? Every single day? New day?! New point!!

Point point point point

I mean that's why we're all here isn't it?

To make yet another point? Out of the deceased, in this case?

Guess it better be a good one!

(*She clears her throat.*)

Wow that snow is really coming down out there isn't it? Isn't each snowflake supposed to be unique? Have you heard that before? Is it true?

(Looking out the window.) If it is true that's a lot of uniqueness just...ceasing to exist.

...

But oh well, we can't be expected to hold funerals for everything.

...

(Rote.) He is survived in death by his wife of fifty-five years, who could have been present today but chose to stay home.

She'll regret, later, that she wasn't here, and she'll probably find a way to blame me for it. Which is understandable. The longer the friendship, the shorter the fuse. Yes?

I'll pass your condolences along to her this afternoon when she returns from her drive. He is also survived by his child, who has a much better excuse for not being here. You see the beloved child of the Old Man Who Never Thought I Would Outlive Him and the Old Woman Who Still Looks Young is headed out of the solar system on a spacecraft bound for a possible Super Earth. We will never know the fate of that mission or its crew.

Godspeed. Very brave choice. Very commendable.

Next up is the burial. I won't be attending myself, however, for any of you that would like to join, or I guess *form* the procession,

There are little orange flags for your car in a basket on top of the piano.

It's a Steinway, I believe. So come have a look, if that matters to you.

And take a flag while you're at it. You can always just not use it. You can even pretend to be driving to the cemetery and then take a "wrong turn" and go home.

You'll get no judgment from me, however you choose to handle it.

Grief is a wild animal that obstinately refuses to explain itself.

...

(She is overcome with emotion.)

I'm sorry but I can't seem to reconcile what is happening, every moment, with all this beautiful snow.

...

THE FUNERAL IS OVER!

(Outside the snow falls heavily.)

Three

(Two snowflakes are falling from the sky. One is a **MOTHER**; *the other is her* **CHILD**.*)*

SNOWFLAKE CHILD. Mom?

MOTHER SNOWFLAKE. Yes, darling?

SNOWFLAKE CHILD. What's consciousness?

MOTHER SNOWFLAKE. Where did you hear that word?!

SNOWFLAKE CHILD. Steven was talking about it.

MOTHER SNOWFLAKE. I told you never to talk to Steven.

SNOWFLAKE CHILD. Sorry, Mom.

MOTHER SNOWFLAKE. …

SNOWFLAKE CHILD. …

MOTHER SNOWFLAKE. …

There are many different philosophies concerning consciousness. We could talk about it our whole lives and never get any closer to understanding it.

Better just to fall.

SNOWFLAKE CHILD. Does it have to do with, like,

Pictures

Or something?

MOTHER SNOWFLAKE. *(Sighs.)* Are you talking about the Big Picture?

SNOWFLAKE CHILD. I think so?

And also the small picture?

MOTHER SNOWFLAKE. The big picture is that we're all going to die.

The small picture is that Steven has bad parents.

SNOWFLAKE CHILD. Okay,

I understand now.

MOTHER SNOWFLAKE. Good.

> (**MOTHER SNOWFLAKE** *begins to move away from her child.*)

Oh, I have to go, Darling.

Destiny is taking me away.

SNOWFLAKE CHILD. What's destiny, Mom?

MOTHER SNOWFLAKE. It's just a different word for wind, dear.

SNOWFLAKE CHILD. Why is destiny blowing you away and not me?

MOTHER SNOWFLAKE. Because it is, sweetheart.

Enjoy the rest of your life.

SNOWFLAKE CHILD. Okay, I will.

MOTHER SNOWFLAKE. Bye, now.

SNOWFLAKE CHILD. Bye.

MOTHER SNOWFLAKE. Darling?

SNOWFLAKE CHILD. Yes, Mom?

MOTHER SNOWFLAKE. There's no one else like you in the whole wide world. And there never will be.

SNOWFLAKE CHILD. Not ever?

MOTHER SNOWFLAKE. Never.

You're the only you there will ever be.

SNOWFLAKE CHILD. Okay.

MOTHER SNOWFLAKE. Darling?

SNOWFLAKE CHILD. Yes, Mom?

MOTHER SNOWFLAKE. When you land,

You may be the final, perfect piece of a puzzle. You may be the one that tips the balance, breaks the branch of a tree.

SNOWFLAKE CHILD. Uhuh.

MOTHER SNOWFLAKE. Or you may be the first white spot on the first flower of spring.

SNOWFLAKE CHILD. Right.

MOTHER SNOWFLAKE. Or you may not be the first. You may be the 1,343rd.

Both numbers are good.

SNOWFLAKE CHILD. Great.

MOTHER SNOWFLAKE. You may land on a child's tongue,

Or a goose's beak.

SNOWFLAKE CHILD. Uhuh.

MOTHER SNOWFLAKE. Or even a sleeping dog's balls.

SNOWFLAKE CHILD. Okay.

MOTHER SNOWFLAKE. No matter where you land, know that I'm proud of you.

SNOWFLAKE CHILD. Thank you, Mom.

MOTHER SNOWFLAKE. Darling?

SNOWFLAKE CHILD. Yeah, Mom?

MOTHER SNOWFLAKE. There are methods to angle yourself away from the dog balls.

SNOWFLAKE CHILD. How?

MOTHER SNOWFLAKE. ...

That's something I can't teach you.

SNOWFLAKE CHILD. ...

MOTHER SNOWFLAKE. It has to do with the way your body is positioned relative to the airstream as you fall.

SNOWFLAKE CHILD. ...

MOTHER SNOWFLAKE. I know how the air passes through me,

But not through you.

You have to discover it for yourself.

SNOWFLAKE CHILD. Okay.

MOTHER SNOWFLAKE. You have to master it for yourself.

SNOWFLAKE CHILD. Got it.

MOTHER SNOWFLAKE. Darling?

SNOWFLAKE CHILD. ...

MOTHER SNOWFLAKE. Darling?

SNOWFLAKE CHILD. *Yeah.*

MOTHER SNOWFLAKE. When I am water again

And you are water again

I will come to you. I will find you.

SNOWFLAKE CHILD. How will you find me?

MOTHER SNOWFLAKE. I am your mother. And that means, sooner or later, I will always find you.

SNOWFLAKE CHILD. ...

MOTHER SNOWFLAKE. Darling.

SNOWFLAKE CHILD. O my God, *what!?*

MOTHER SNOWFLAKE. I know life can feel long sometimes. But it isn't long at all.

SNOWFLAKE CHILD. I thought you were leaving.

MOTHER SNOWFLAKE. So did I, but the wind has calmed a bit.

SNOWFLAKE CHILD. …

> (**SNOWFLAKE CHILD** *looks down toward the ground far below.*)

MOTHER SNOWFLAKE. What are you thinking about?

SNOWFLAKE CHILD. …

Consciousness.

…

I'm sorry, Mom.

MOTHER SNOWFLAKE. Don't be sorry.

…

I think,

I think there actually *is* a simple way to explain it, darling.

SNOWFLAKE CHILD. …

Will you tell it to me?

MOTHER SNOWFLAKE. I suppose that's my duty, isn't it?

SNOWFLAKE CHILD. …

MOTHER SNOWFLAKE. Okay, so basically –

> (*Destiny blows* **MOTHER SNOWFLAKE** *far, far away.*)

> (**SNOWFLAKE CHILD** *looks at the ground far below.*)

Four

(Outside the house. In the garden. There are wildflowers everywhere.)

*(**MAN** enters. He's on the phone. It's a business call.)*

MAN. Yeah.

…

Yeah.

…

Yeah.

…

No.

…

No.

…

Definitely no.

…

Uhuh.

…

Uhuh.

…

No.

…

I'm out.

…

Yeah,

No.

…

Soulless enterprise.

Not interested.

 (**JUNIOR** *enters.*)

…

I can call in next Monday if they need…

…

I appreciate that.

…

How's the family?

…

Good, we're good.

Can't complain.

No complaining in the Spring. That's the rule around here.

…

No, yeah, we're making it work. We see people. Had a group over for dinner last night.

…

Oh, you know it was.

…

Yeah they grow up too fast.

 (**MAN** *exits.*)

 (**JUNIOR** *stares at the ground.*)

> (**WOMAN** *comes out the front door of the house with gardening tools.*)

WOMAN. Hello, child of mine. Something on your mind?

JUNIOR. Yeah.

WOMAN. Anything you want to talk about?

JUNIOR. Not particularly.

WOMAN. Alright, then, do you want to help me weed? We have some volunteer tomatoes this year.

JUNIOR. Volunteer?

WOMAN. Wild tomato plants! Come look.

> (*The* **GOOSE** *enters. She bites her feathers occasionally and looks around, taking little interest in* **WOMAN** *or* **JUNIOR**.)

JUNIOR. But they're not *actually* volunteering. They don't even know we exist.

WOMAN. ...

Something going on, honey?

JUNIOR. Are we part of the global elite?

WOMAN. The what?

No. No, of course not. What made you ask that?

JUNIOR. I kind of feel like we are.

WOMAN. Well to tell you the truth I don't quite know what you mean by "global elite."

JUNIOR. What's Dad doing right now?

WOMAN. He's on the phone with our property manager in Hong Kong. Or Brazil. One of the two.

Listen. Honey. We are grateful for what we have. We try our / best to –

JUNIOR. Why can't you just tell me the truth?

WOMAN. You interrupted me.

JUNIOR. Apologies.

WOMAN. One apology is plenty. Never over-apologize.

JUNIOR. …

Well maybe I'm sorry for more than one thing.

WOMAN. What else are you sorry for?

JUNIOR. …

Not turning out the way you wanted me to.

WOMAN. Honey, you're twelve.

JUNIOR. Yeah but it's not like I'm gonna *change.*

WOMAN. …

JUNIOR. I'm saying like personality wise… I'm not gonna, like, turn into a gardener.

WOMAN. Honey, did you think…did you think I wanted you to be exactly like me?

JUNIOR. Yeah. Kind of.

WOMAN. No. No not at all. I want you to learn about gardening because it's a valuable thing to know. I *wish* I had discovered it earlier. That doesn't mean I'm expecting you to inherit this garden.

JUNIOR. Are you sure?

WOMAN. …

What's bringing this on?

JUNIOR. I don't know, okay?!

I'm sorry!

WOMAN. Hey,

It's okay.

Try not to put too much pressure on yourself. You still have so much growing up to do. When I was your age, I thought it was my destiny to be a doctor. It seemed to make perfect sense. My mother is a nurse. And my father is a medical technician.

JUNIOR. Mom, no offense, but I know.

WOMAN. But you don't. You don't know what it meant to them when I got into medical school.

You didn't see the looks on their faces when I told them. Giving them the news was, to that point, the highlight of my life. Did I ever tell you that?

JUNIOR. Yeah Mom, you tell me this on like a fortnightly basis.

WOMAN. Well, it's a true story. That look on their faces was the high point of my young life. And it took me a long time to realize that, deep down, I just didn't care about medicine. Not enough to want to practice it, at any rate.

JUNIOR. *(Impatient.)* And you never had the heart to tell Grandma and Grandpa that you were dropping out of med school, so you let them figure it out on their own, and you still feel bad about it.

WOMAN. …

…

I'm sorry to bore you.

I guess the reason I keep saying it is that I'm not at peace with my decision.

I guess I've gotten a little evangelical about gardening because I'm still trying to convince myself that it's the right thing. That it's a worthy use of my time.

The last thing I wanted to do was burden you with my own issues.

I never want you to worry that you'll disappoint me.

The only thing that would disappoint me,

Is if you didn't follow your own heart.

…

Wow, I need to relax. You're twelve! I'm sorry.

It's not that serious.

JUNIOR. I mean, I'm twelve right now, but so what? Time is malleable. I'll remember this. I'll use it when I need it.

WOMAN. Well,

Good.

> (**JUNIOR** *begins to leave.*)

Where are you going, honey?

JUNIOR. Away.

WOMAN. Away where?

JUNIOR. I don't know. Maybe to a place where people actually live up to their professed ideals.

WOMAN. Excuse me?

JUNIOR. I'm sorry, I have a lot of feelings about a lot of things and sometimes I get really mad!

WOMAN. We'll talk about it at dinner.

You're excused.

JUNIOR. I don't want to talk about it.

WOMAN. When you're going through big emotions, we talk about them. Even when it's hard.

JUNIOR. The talking is what makes it hard.

WOMAN. That's an interesting thought.

I'll keep that in mind.

JUNIOR. Ughhhhhhhhh!

(**JUNIOR** *exits.*)

(**WOMAN** *looks at* **GOOSE.**)

GOOSE. Twelve to twenty-two. It's a tough span. You're doing good.

WOMAN. Do *you* like the gardens?

GOOSE. Yeah, sure. I've gotten used to them.

They're nice. In their own unique way.

WOMAN. We had a wonderful dinner party last night.

The house was full of people.

And laughter.

GOOSE. Yeah. Sounded like a lot of fun.

WOMAN. People kept asking me what I *did.*

What do you do?

I never know how to answer that question.

I usually say: *I have a background in medicine, but I've moved in another direction.* And then they say,

Oh?

And then I say...well it depends.

Yesterday, we were home – so it was easy. I just took people out here.

And I talked about how breathing in this air is so so good for our health and our well-being,

And how cities are wonderful places but they are also terrible places, simply by virtue of what they were designed to do, which is innovate innovate innovate ad nauseam, grow grow grow but we're growing ourselves out of our own clothes, and the solution isn't always *make new clothes,* we need to learn new ways of being, which are also old ways of being, and embracing our limitations has to be part of the equation, because the ferns and the flowers, not to mention the rocks and the mountains, and the continental plates, have things to teach us, and old lessons can be a source of new wisdom, and things we never thought possible are possible because they've been hiding in plain sight but we'll never discover them unless we foster the patience to breathe them in,

And by the end of it,

By the end of my speech,

Or maybe it was more of a lecture,

I looked at everyone's faces and most of them were... well they were smiling. Politely.

And suddenly I felt so foolish.

I felt like a long-winded tour guide at the tail end of a presentation that nobody asked for.

(**GOOSE** *bites her feathers.*)

I guess I have to admit to myself that, as much as I think I should be in the prime of my life, I still haven't figured out...um,

Life.

GOOSE. Yeah.

You know, you reminded me of something.

Thank you.

WOMAN. What did I remind you of?

GOOSE. ...

I'm not really a goose.

WOMAN. ...

GOOSE. I mean, yes, I'm a *goose.*

In the sense that I'm, *becoming one.*

Because that's the way people perceive me.

Because *goose* fits within their frame of reference.

So, in the process of taking on that mantle, I've been... shrinking.

But, originally, I was something else.

WOMAN. Oh.

GOOSE. My mother was a...

I'm not sure if there's an English word for it.

She was a

> *(The* **GOOSE** *honks.)*

So, naturally, that's what I was, too. When I was born. You know, eons ago.

WOMAN. I see.

GOOSE. But you know how it is. If you want to survive, you adapt. You evolve.

And goose is definitely the direction I'm headed.

I mean it isn't really up to me, but yeah. That's the final destination, I think.

On this plane of existence.

...

So.

Tell me about your wedding.

WOMAN. Why?

GOOSE. Because I just told you something about my origins. And I want to know about yours.

WOMAN. A wedding isn't an origin. It's –

GOOSE. Well nothing is *really* an origin. Except, you know, The Origin. But when you begin a new life...by which I mean, you know, when you decide to walk a new kind of path...

　　　*(***GOOSE*** *produces a wedding dress.)*

You left this in the barn.

　　　...

WOMAN. Oh.

GOOSE. It's beautiful. Why would you leave it in a building you so rarely enter?

WOMAN. ...

GOOSE. Try it on.

　　　*(***GOOSE*** *bites her feathers.)*

　　　*(***WOMAN*** *puts on her wedding dress and travels approximately fifteen years backward through the space-time continuum. It is the day of her wedding.)*

　　　(The yard becomes a forest clearing. The ***GOOSE****, if still present, retreats to the perimeter of the playing space.)*

　　　*(***WOMAN*** *pulls out her phone. She begins looking around for her fiancé.)*

　　　(A ***GRAY-BEARDED MAN*** *jumps out of the bushes.)*

GRAY-BEARDED MAN. Are you here for a wedding!?

WOMAN. AH!

GRAY-BEARDED MAN. You have a look in your eyes as if
you're about to get married. Is it true?

WOMAN. Yes. No.

I'm reliving my wedding day – but I don't think you're
supposed to be here.

GRAY-BEARDED MAN. Why not?

WOMAN. Who are you?

GRAY-BEARDED MAN. Oh, I don't use a name anymore.

Cumbersome.

When does the wedding start?

WOMAN. As soon as my fiancé gets here.

GRAY-BEARDED MAN. You're eloping?

WOMAN. Not exactly.

GRAY-BEARDED MAN. Then why are there no witnesses?

No family?

WOMAN. We just want it to be for us.

Between us.

Just us and a promise.

GRAY-BEARDED MAN. Oh.

That's a terrible mistake.

Love is a fire.

Love is very dangerous. You need people around who
can help keep you safe from it.

WOMAN. I don't want to hear that right now.

GRAY-BEARDED MAN. Why not?

You seem to be the kind of person who wants to know the truth.

WOMAN. Will you please go back to wherever you came from?

GRAY-BEARDED MAN. Okay.

(**GRAY-BEARDED MAN** *returns to the bushes.*)

(From bushes.) I hope you don't mind if I watch the wedding from here.

Oh. And I should mention that the vows you've written, unfortunately, won't prove adequate. They'll be just fine for today, of course. But they won't hold up for the duration.

WOMAN. How do you know?

GRAY-BEARDED MAN. *(From bushes.)* In a past life, I was a detective.

Old habits die hard, as they say. In fact, most habits live longer than people. Much longer.

WOMAN. That's very interesting, but I'm not sure what you think you know about my vows.

GRAY-BEARDED MAN. I don't speak as someone who holds secret knowledge, but as a friend. Which is to say, someone who listens and observes. Listen to and observe all the world, and you can be a friend to all the world. Be a friend to all the world, and the world will share with you its ever-renewing life.

Oh, here he comes!

(**MAN** *enters. He's disheveled and limping.*)

MAN. Hey.

WOMAN. Are you okay!?

MAN. Yeah, of course. Sorry I was here earlier and you weren't so I went looking.

WOMAN. ...

MAN. You are radiant.

Ouch.

Sorry, I twisted my ankle.

WOMAN. Again?

MAN. Yeah it just rolled. These shoes aren't made for walks in the woods.

WOMAN. Well, you twist your ankle a lot.

You've twisted it in pretty much every pair of shoes you own.

MAN. You're right

...

You're right.

>   (**MAN** *removes his shoes.*)

All these things. These possessions. These earthly trappings.

>   (*He removes his socks. And his pants.*)

WOMAN. What is happening?

MAN. I don't want anything to come between us.

>   (*He removes his shirt.*)

Just you. And just me. And this forest. And a promise that will last forever.

>   (*He removes his underwear.*)

>   (*The bushes, perhaps, move in to cover him.*)

>   (*He is now completely naked.*)

WOMAN. ...

This is all going so badly.

Maybe it's a sign. Maybe we shouldn't get married.

GRAY-BEARDED MAN. *(From trees.)* Wedding's off, you say? Over one small misunderstanding?

WOMAN. SHUT UP!!

MAN. Why are you screaming at the trees?

WOMAN. Because the trees are interrupting!

MAN. Come on.

Take off your beautiful dress.

WOMAN. ...

I'm going to keep my dress on.

> (**WOMAN** *takes a deep breath.*)

> *(She picks up her phone.)*

MAN. What are you doing?

WOMAN. Getting my vows.

MAN. ...

WOMAN. Didn't you make vows?

MAN. Like, ahead of time? No way.

I wanted to speak from the heart.

WOMAN. ...

So did I. Which is why I *prepared.*

MAN. I love you.

WOMAN. ...

MAN. I love you like time loves the clock.

I love you / like the wind loves the water,

Like the water loves the mineral kingdom,

Like the sand loves the salt of the ocean,

Like the reef loves the animals that live in it.

WOMAN. What?

> *(Mosquitos start biting the* **WOMAN**. *She slaps at them.)*

MAN. What are you doing?

WOMAN. Mosquitos.

MAN. ...

Let me know when you're ready for me to continue.

WOMAN. *(Continuing to slap mosquitos.)* I'm listening, go ahead.

MAN. From the moment I saw you, I saw a life with you.

I wanted to fly a kite with you.

I wanted to see the sights with you.

> *(The mosquitos are getting worse and worse.)*

WOMAN. Are they not biting you at all?

MAN. They can have as much of my blood as they want.

My heart will make more.

WOMAN. Are you done with the vows?

Or is there more?

MAN. ...

I'm done. You go.

WOMAN. Okay,

> *(Reading from her phone.)*

I've never known anyone like you.

And I never thought I would.

If I'm being honest, you're not what I envisioned.

When I dreamt of my future husband.

You are not the man of my dreams.

You are the man of my reality.

You have taught me more

About myself

 (She's getting choked up.)

...

More about myself

...

I'm sorry.

...

You've taught me more about myself,

Than I ever thought there was to know.

And there's nothing in the world I want more than to keep learning and growing with you.

 (She slaps a mosquito, but doesn't miss a beat.)

I want to be the version of myself

That has a life with you.

A whole life.

And life is long, even though at times it seems very short.

 *(The bushes take **WOMAN**'s phone and hand her a piece of paper.)*

 *(**WOMAN** reads from the piece of paper.)*

"As we get older, things that are simple will become more complicated.

And the things that once brought us pleasure will bring us pain."

...

Will you bring me pain?

...

MAN. I hope not.

WOMAN. Will I bring you pain?

MAN. Well if you do, I'll forgive you. I'm sure it won't be on purpose.

      *(***WOMAN*** laughs.)*

      (She remembers why she loves and trusts him so much.)

WOMAN. I love you.

      *(The ***GRAY-BEARDED MAN*** comes out from behind the bushes and gives ***MAN*** his clothes.)*

      *(***MAN*** puts his clothes back on.)*

      *(***WOMAN*** and ***MAN*** look at each other.)*

I do not have a ring.

But with these words

I wed thee.

GRAY-BEARDED MAN. How beautiful.

MAN. I do not have a ring,

But with these words

I wed thee.

(**GRAY-BEARDED MAN** *exits.*)

(*It begins to snow.*)

(**MAN** *exits.*)

(**GOOSE** *enters.*)

(*Lights shift. We're outside the house again.*)

GOOSE. Wow.

WOMAN. Yeah.

We were impossibly naïve.

GOOSE. There's this saying we have:

(**GOOSE** *honks three times.*)

Let the mockingbirds bleed internally as they shit themselves with laughter. Is the direct translation. But the sense of it is like...*don't ridicule yourself.*

WOMAN. A little self-deprecation never hurt anyone.

GOOSE. I hope you don't judge your child as ruthlessly as you judge yourself.

WOMAN. ...

GOOSE. There's beauty and truth in the rashness of youth.

WOMAN. I need to get dinner ready.

(**WOMAN** *picks some tomatoes, then goes into the house.*)

(**GOOSE** *bites her feathers.*)

Five

(*Inside their house,* **WOMAN**, **MAN**, *and* **JUNIOR** *sit around the table.*)

JUNIOR. May I be excused?

WOMAN. We just sat down.

JUNIOR. I ate.

MAN. Ate what? Your food is right there.

JUNIOR. I'm not hungry.

MAN. Okay, well that's different. That's a different conversation.

JUNIOR. Ugh.

MAN. Pass the green beans please.

JUNIOR. Why?

MAN. ...

WOMAN. Pass your father the green beans.

(**JUNIOR** *passes the green beans, with attitude.*)

MAN. What's going on?

JUNIOR. I'm passing you the green beans that you asked for.

WOMAN. Put them back. Try again.

JUNIOR. Oh my God.

(**JUNIOR** *puts the green beans back and passes them again. With slightly less attitude.*)

MAN. ...

WOMAN. Would you like to tell your father about the talk we had outside?

>   (**JUNIOR** *eats.*)

MAN. So you talked, huh?

WOMAN. We talked about a lot of things, didn't we?

JUNIOR. ...

WOMAN. We were wondering what your phone calls were about today.

MAN. Oh, yeah, I was talking to our property manager in Greenland.

JUNIOR. You have property in Greenland?

MAN. *We* have property in Greenland. Which, by the way, you will inherit someday.

JUNIOR. I don't believe in owning property.

MAN. ...

Okay. Noted.

Anyway, I was talking to the manager of our Greenland properties, and she's gotten us to carbon negative.

WOMAN. Oh, that's wonderful!

MAN. Yeah, I know, she really deserves all the credit – I mean, I gave the directive, but she's the one that made it happen. And so, now, I'm trying to get some investors together to start up a consulting firm, which she would run, with the goal of... I know this is ambitious... making *Greenland as a whole* carbon negative.

WOMAN. NO WAY!!

MAN. I think it's possible. Gotta aim big, the future of the world is at stake.

JUNIOR. So do you think you're a hero now? Because you made a phone call?

WOMAN. ...

Child of mine...

JUNIOR. Sorry, Dad.

WOMAN. ...

JUNIOR. What?

WOMAN. That is not acceptable.

JUNIOR. I said I was sorry.

WOMAN. You, my child, are the heart of my heart.

And because of that, because of how much I love you, There are no small battles here. There is no letting go. There is no compromise. You will show proper respect. And if you do not, I will fight you, and I will never give up. I will torment you until I win.

JUNIOR. Got it. So I'm not allowed to disagree with you guys. That seems a little tyrannical but whatever I'll just undermine you in subtle ways for a few years and completely rebel when I'm seventeen.

WOMAN. What is it exactly that you disagree with?

JUNIOR. Your sense of justice. Or lack thereof.

MAN. ...

Carbon *negative*. It's a good thing. It means we're extracting more carbon from the atmosphere than we're putting into it.

JUNIOR. I'm talking about the fact that I didn't want to be at this table. So I asked to be excused. Which is a rule that only applies to me, by the way, you guys can leave the table whenever you want, but whatever –

MAN. Well let me ask you this: have you ever seen us leave the table without touching our food?

JUNIOR. No, I haven't. That's why I said whatever. 'Cause it's whatever.

MAN. ...

JUNIOR. I get an attitude sometimes, okay, like excuse me for being on the cusp of puberty.

WOMAN. Your feelings are not the problem, honey. The problem is that you're not telling us what's really bothering you.

JUNIOR. YOU are bothering me! I can't deal with these dinners! Like I really can't. It's just, all these formalities. And you want to sit here and congratulate yourselves about Greenland, like what about your actual home? What about the fact that Mrs. Goose is out there, hungry, just staring in the window!?

> *(All turn to the window. The* **GOOSE**, *who has indeed been staring in, turns away and pretends to be staring somewhere else.)*

MAN. *Mrs.* Goose?

WOMAN. …

MAN. She's not a member of the family.

JUNIOR. Depends on your definition of family, I guess.

MAN. Well…*our* definition of family…

WOMAN. …

MAN. Would be the three of us. Okay. And then that extends out to your grandparents, okay? And your aunts and uncles and cousins and so on and so forth.

WOMAN. Would you mind sharing with us what your definition of family is?

JUNIOR. All the beings in a given ecosystem.

WOMAN. That's a very interesting way of looking at it.

MAN. So then, the ecosystem…does it have borders of any kind? Or does it just, kind of, extend indefinitely?

JUNIOR. Ecosystems aren't about borders. Ecosystems are about relationships.

MAN. Right.

Okay, then.

JUNIOR. May I *please* be excused –

WOMAN. We're in the middle of a conversation –

JUNIOR. How is this a conversation!?

MAN. When two or more people talk to each other, that's generally called a conversation. Then again, I don't know what *your* definition of a conversation is.

JUNIOR. I don't think the way you think, I don't believe what you believe and yet, every night, at dinner, you insist that we sit across from each other so you can lecture me about the way *you see the world.*

That's not a conversation. That's indoctrination. And I'm so sick of it. I can't believe that I have to somehow *prove* to you that Mrs. Goose experiences emotions.

MAN. The goose, I thought we explained this to you, the goose was never ours. She was here when we moved in –

JUNIOR. Exactly. And since she's not *yours,* since you don't *own* her, you're not *invested* in her well-being.

Right?

How could you be? Unless you run a cost-benefit analysis and discover that caring is less expensive. Which it probably is.

MAN. What are you talking about, / you're losing me –

JUNIOR. I'm talking about the fact that you and Mom are out here living a colonizer fever dream, and you think you're so enlightened, but you're not, all you're concerned about is what you can *claim,* what you can *own,* what you can *take credit for,* what you can *extract value* from. If you really cared about Mrs. Goose, if you really respected her as a conscious, aware, living

being, and if this daily meal ritual is truly something
you think is important, then you would invite her in.
You would sit down and eat with her.

MAN. ...

WOMAN. ...

JUNIOR. But you can't even like, fathom that. Can you?
That idea is so impossible to you. So *foreign* to you, you
can barely even process it. What does it *mean*? That's
what you want to know. What does it *mean*. Which is
another way of saying: What do I get from it?

How do I benefit? What's in it for *me*. How about
asking a different question? How about asking, "How
does this meal honor the interconnectedness of all life
forms?"

How about asking, "Did I fulfill my purpose today? Did
I? If not, maybe I shouldn't be eating another life-form
to fuel my utter uselessness. Maybe I should spend that
time meditating, and centering myself, so I can have a
better day tomorrow!"

And I just, I don't understand. I don't understand
how you can tell me to be good, and then not be good
yourselves,

And then get mad at me for not being perfect,

And Mrs. Goose is probably hungry,

May I be excused to feed her please?

MAN. ...

WOMAN. ...

Bring her in.

MAN. ...

JUNIOR. Seriously?

MAN. Hold on.

WOMAN. Points were articulated.

Honest feelings were expressed.

MAN. Okay, listen this is all...

I respect a lot of what's been said here. This has been a very good, very enlightening conversation. You know *this* is why we do insist on having dinner together. So things don't fester. So conversations can happen.

But, uh,

You know there are lines that have to be drawn.

JUNIOR. Of course there are.

I knew that's what you'd say.

WOMAN. ...

MAN. ...

Fine. Bring her in.

> (**JUNIOR** *opens the door, looks at* **GOOSE.** *The* **GOOSE** *meanders around for a while.* **JUNIOR** *motions for* **GOOSE** *to come inside.*)

GOOSE. I'm sorry, what?

JUNIOR. Come on in, Mrs. Goose. Are you hungry?

GOOSE. I'm sorry, what? What's happening?

JUNIOR. It's okay, come on in. We're having dinner. You do such a great job guarding the house every day. You deserve a warm dinner more than any of us.

GOOSE. I mean...okay? I don't really, uh...

> (**GOOSE** *enters the house.*)

Alright, it's pretty weird in here. Glad I could make it. Can I go now?

JUNIOR. Come here to the table. You can have my seat.

GOOSE. I'm supposed to sit there?

...

Okay.

Here I am. This is weird. Hi everyone.

MAN. ...

She doesn't look very happy.

GOOSE. I'm happy I'm just a little...never mind.

What's for dinner, what is this?

WOMAN. So, uh, we have some green beans here. And some mashed potatoes. And some chicken.

GOOSE. Chicken. Okay, that's a little close to home but I think I can work with it.

JUNIOR. Please eat, if you're hungry, Mrs. Goose.

GOOSE. Just kind of...eat? Like eat it?

Eat the food? ...

...

> (**GOOSE**, *suddenly, forcefully, violently, begins pecking at the food. She slams her face onto the table repeatedly, knocking dishes everywhere.*)
>
> (*This lasts for a long time, until all the food is eaten or destroyed.*)

Can I go back outside now?

> (**GOOSE** *exits.*)

JUNIOR. I'm sorry.

I'll clean it up.

Sorry Mom.

Sorry Dad.

MAN. That was my great-grandmother's china set.

>(**MAN** *exits.*)

WOMAN. He'll be okay.

>...

>It's just...stuff.

JUNIOR. ...

>...

>(**JUNIOR** *starts cleaning up the mess.* **WOMAN** *looks on without moving much.*)

WOMAN. ...

You might want to sweep the glass rather than trying to pick it up.

JUNIOR. Okay, Mom.

>(**WOMAN** *hands* **JUNIOR** *a broom and dustpan.*)

>(**JUNIOR**, *devastated, continues cleaning up.*)

WOMAN. You're going to do wonderful, wonderful things in the world. There is nothing wrong with your passion. There is nothing wrong with your conviction.

JUNIOR. ...But?

WOMAN. ...

But nothing.

>...

I love you.

>(**WOMAN** *exits.*)

ACT TWO

Six

(*A ski chalet.*)

(**GRAY-BEARDED MAN** *sits alone.*)

(*Outside the large window are snow-covered mountains.*)

(**WOMAN** *enters, wearing a ski suit. She is out of breath.*)

(**WOMAN** *sits on the other side of the room from* **GRAY-BEARDED MAN**. *She unzips her ski suit.*)

(*She fans herself off with her hands.*)

(*She makes a conscious effort to slow her breathing and her heart rate.*)

(**GRAY-BEARDED MAN** *looks at her.*)

GRAY-BEARDED MAN. ...

WOMAN. I'm fine.

I'm okay.

GRAY-BEARDED MAN. Glad to hear it!

WOMAN. Just a little brush with death.

No big deal.

GRAY-BEARDED MAN. Those can be hard to avoid.

WOMAN. I wouldn't recommend skiing alone. Especially if you're doing it for the first time.

GRAY-BEARDED MAN. Alone?

(**GRAY-BEARDED MAN** *laughs.*)

WOMAN. …

GRAY-BEARDED MAN. Oh. I'm not mocking you.

I don't subscribe to the concept of aloneness. At least, as conventionally understood.

WOMAN. …

GRAY-BEARDED MAN. So, your trip down the mountain wasn't what you expected?

WOMAN. Not at all.

And never again.

GRAY-BEARDED MAN. What inspired it? If you don't mind my asking.

WOMAN. I wanted to try something new. To remind myself that I'm still young.

GRAY-BEARDED MAN. …

WOMAN. My only child went off to college last weekend.

GRAY-BEARDED MAN. Oh, congratulations!

WOMAN. It happened so fast. So much life went by so quickly.

GRAY-BEARDED MAN. You sound like you have regrets.

WOMAN. I don't think I did enough. For my child. And now I can't do much of anything.

GRAY-BEARDED MAN.　Well, doing enough, that's impossible with children. There's a lot they have to do on their own.

WOMAN.　Do you have children?

GRAY-BEARDED MAN.　I have a few.

WOMAN.　How are they doing?

GRAY-BEARDED MAN.　Some are doing better than others.

Then again, I don't really know that for sure.

They might all be doing equally well, relative to what's possible for them.

The ones that I think are doing the best may be doing the worst. Or they may not. I just love them now. That's all I can do at this stage, fortunately or unfortunately.

WOMAN.　Right.

Well, good. Sounds like you've figured it out.

> (**GRAY-BEARDED MAN** *walks to* **WOMAN** *and sits next to her.*)

GRAY-BEARDED MAN.　I have, actually.

WOMAN.　...

GRAY-BEARDED MAN.　Do you mind if I join you?

WOMAN.　Go right ahead.

GRAY-BEARDED MAN.　Thank you.

WOMAN.　...

You were saying?

GRAY-BEARDED MAN.　Oh.

Yes.

Life. I've figured it out.

WOMAN.　Okay...

GRAY-BEARDED MAN. Time isn't relative.

WOMAN. ...

GRAY-BEARDED MAN. A clock: relative.

A year: relative.

A century: relative.

Time itself?

Absolute.

WOMAN. ...

Cool.

GRAY-BEARDED MAN. We did not invent time. Time gave birth to us. It's the fundamental law of existence. And it's been with us all along. All we have to do: is admit it.

WOMAN. Admit what?

GRAY-BEARDED MAN. That we're not the center of the universe.

And then we'll find that everything,

Everything,

Is resolved.

...

That's why, even when I'm facing the specter of doubt, I'm fundamentally happy.

WOMAN. There are a lot of crumbs on your...

> (**WOMAN** *makes a brushing motion with her hands across her chest to indicate that* **GRAY-BEARDED MAN** *should brush himself off.*)

> (*He looks at the crumbs but does not brush himself off.*)

GRAY-BEARDED MAN. That's only a muffin from my breakfast.

WOMAN. Oh.

GRAY-BEARDED MAN. Does it bother you?

WOMAN. It's a lot of crumbs.

GRAY-BEARDED MAN. Muffins are crumbly. It's their nature. Nothing to be done. If I were wearing a shirt with the likeness of a muffin printed upon it, what would you say?

WOMAN. I don't know.

GRAY-BEARDED MAN. More than likely you'd say, "nice shirt."

I know because I own such a shirt. And almost everyone who sees it says "nice shirt." In fact, if I'm lucky, I may be wearing it now.

(He removes his jacket. He is, indeed, wearing the shirt.)

WOMAN. That *is* a nice shirt.

GRAY-BEARDED MAN. Yes, I know.

The real muffin offends you.

The illusion pleases you.

The illusion of a muffin, you see, is a statement. It seems to say, "Muffins: I like them. And I know that I like them. I am an intelligent being. I am aware of myself. If you are an intelligent and aware being like me, smile or laugh or say *nice shirt* and we'll share not a muffin, but something higher. Thus, we connect. Even if for a short time, we bond. Speaking of which, why isn't your husband with you?"

WOMAN. ...

I don't know what you think you know about my husband.

GRAY-BEARDED MAN. Neither do I. That's why I asked.

WOMAN. …

Our child went off to college, and I wanted to go on a trip.

But we have a…pet.

That has become almost like a member of the family.

And my husband had to stay home to feed it.

GRAY-BEARDED MAN. So,

Your love has matured. You allow each other the space to grow in your own respective spheres. But you are ever connected.

How beautiful.

WOMAN. Thanks.

GRAY-BEARDED MAN. We're all evolving together. Aren't we?

Human beings, I mean.

Technology and travel are changing us.

We're becoming a new thing.

Have you noticed?

Our kids are going to be just

Light-years ahead. Literally.

I mean that literally.

They are going to be *out there*.

Our children.

WOMAN. Yes, I'm afraid so.

GRAY-BEARDED MAN. Well, what can we old ones do?

WOMAN. I'd like to hope we can watch them grow up.

And work alongside them.

And keep helping them.

For as long as possible.

GRAY-BEARDED MAN. And what else can we do?

WOMAN. I actually thought that was a pretty good answer.

GRAY-BEARDED MAN. It's a fine answer.

But it's certainly not *the* answer.

WOMAN. What is *the* answer?

GRAY-BEARDED MAN. I don't believe it exists.

WOMAN. Okay, so then what are you expecting out of this conversation?

GRAY-BEARDED MAN. I'm expecting to get…within orbit

Of the truth.

WOMAN. What's that sticking out of your jacket pocket?

GRAY-BEARDED MAN. …

WOMAN. The jacket behind you.

> (**GRAY-BEARDED MAN** *looks over his shoulder, as if expecting the jacket to be standing behind him.*)

GRAY-BEARDED MAN. Jacket?

WOMAN. The jacket on your chair. The one you just took off to show me your stupid shirt –

GRAY-BEARDED MAN. I thought you liked my shirt.

WOMAN. I do but I'm irritated –

GRAY-BEARDED MAN. Why? –

WOMAN. Because you're acting like you don't know there's a jacket draped over your chair –

GRAY-BEARDED MAN. There are a lot of things I don't know. / I don't like to dwell on them.

WOMAN. What's that in the pocket?

>(**GRAY-BEARDED MAN** *finally sees the jacket.*)

GRAY-BEARDED MAN. Oh, this?

It's a potion that will extend your life by fifty years.

There are some people who, wherever they go, have a galvanizing effect on their environment. Those people, I think, should live a little longer. Learn more. See more.

Touch more of the soil.

Not for their own sake, but for the sake of our planet. And our civilization.

WOMAN. ...

GRAY-BEARDED MAN. That's what the bartender told me, anyway. Not a bad line.

WOMAN. How many of those does the bartender have?

GRAY-BEARDED MAN. Not sure.

This is a free sample. The bartender promised I would feel the effects and want to come back for more.

WOMAN. Each bottle extends your life fifty years? It's cumulative?

GRAY-BEARDED MAN. The bartender didn't exactly specify. But if I had to guess I'd say, no. Probably not. I'm sure if I do come back for more I'll be sold a whole regimen. A whole way of life.

>(**GRAY-BEARDED MAN** *hands the bottle to* **WOMAN.**)

>(*She examines it, smells it.*)

WOMAN. It smells like...rose water?

GRAY-BEARDED MAN. That may be all it is. Would you like to split it?

I'm sure it's nonsense but we can taste it and pretend.

WOMAN. I'll buy my own.

Nice to talk with you.

(**WOMAN** *exits abruptly.*)

Seven

(Inside the house.)

*(**MAN** sits alone.)*

*(The door opens and the **GOOSE** enters.)*

GOOSE. You haven't fed me in a while.

MAN. Sorry, I've been distracted.

GOOSE. It doesn't take very long.

MAN. Sorry.

GOOSE. Should I just –

I mean I can fend for myself. It's not a problem.

I just kind of need to know.

'Cause if you're going to feed me

That just changes my plan.

That changes the structure of my day.

So it's not –

I don't even need you to feed me.

I just need to know if you're going to feed me.

MAN. I'll let you know. I'll let you know real soon.

GOOSE. That's actually the worst possible answer.

That keeps me in an indefinite holding pattern.

Which is the thing I'm trying to avoid.

Which is the reason I came in here.

MAN. …

GOOSE. I'm just going to assume

That you aren't going to feed me.

I'm going to assume

That you're going to keep sitting in that chair until you die.

MAN. …

GOOSE. And so it's up to me.

In terms of eating.

That's the assumption I'm operating on.

MAN. …

GOOSE. So if at any point you believe that assumption to be incorrect,

Please let me know.

Okay?

MAN. …

Sure thing.

GOOSE. Thanks.

MAN. No problem.

GOOSE. Do I look shorter to you?

MAN. …

GOOSE. I feel noticeably shorter.

I think it's really happening.

I think I'm starting to get old.

…

I don't think I like it.

(**GOOSE** *exits.*)

MAN. Call Junior.

(The walls of the house wake up.)

VOICE. Calling your child.

(The sound of a phone ringing.)

*(**JUNIOR** answers.)*

JUNIOR. Hey Dad.

MAN. Hey there.

JUNIOR. What's up?

MAN. Not much how's school?

JUNIOR. Good.

MAN. How are my old stomping grounds?

JUNIOR. Good.

MAN. Do people use that term anymore? Stomping grounds?

JUNIOR. Not really but I know what you mean.

MAN. It's good, huh?

Can you feel my ghost walking around there?

JUNIOR. Uhhh, that's kind of a weird thing to say, Dad.

MAN. Why?

JUNIOR. You're not dead.

MAN. Well I don't see why I should wait 'til I'm dead just to haunt a place.

It's not as if I'm going back there.

JUNIOR. Well I guess in that sense, I'm your ghost.

MAN. Yeah.

So how's it going?

JUNIOR. Good.

MAN. Are you thinking about studying abroad at all?

JUNIOR. Uhhh. I mean no.

MAN. You should maybe consider...

JUNIOR. ...

Dad?

MAN. Consider Antarctica.

Consider Mars also.

JUNIOR. Dad, are you alright?

MAN. Consider places that people haven't corrupted.

And consider going there

And just

Standing guard.

Standing guard

And not letting anybody near.

Not letting anybody close.

And fighting to the death

For the sanctity of creation.

JUNIOR. Is Mom there?

MAN. No she's on a trip.

JUNIOR. By herself?

MAN. She's an adult she can travel by herself.

JUNIOR. Why didn't you go with her?

You guys always go places together.

MAN. She'll be back soon.

JUNIOR. I'm gonna give her a call.

MAN. She wants to live to be one hundred and fifty.

JUNIOR. I know, there's no reason why she shouldn't. I think I'll be able to get close to two hundred.

MAN. Yeah.

JUNIOR. That's what we always say, Dad.

MAN. I know.

JUNIOR. I'm gonna let you go and I'm gonna call Mom.

MAN. Okay.

JUNIOR. Unless you want me to try to get her on the line.

MAN. No no. I'll see her when she gets back.

JUNIOR. Thanks for calling, Dad.

MAN. You're welcome, thanks for answering.

JUNIOR. Talk to you soon.

MAN. Okay.

	…

JUNIOR. Bye.

MAN. …

	…

Bye, talk to you soon.

> (**MAN** *sits in his chair.*)

> (*He looks out the window.*)

> (**WOMAN** *and* **GOOSE** *enter.*)

Oh.

Hey.

WOMAN. How long have you been sitting there?

MAN. Not sure.

(**WOMAN** *gestures toward* **GOOSE.**)

WOMAN. Look what's happened.

GOOSE. ...

MAN. I'm sorry?

WOMAN. *Are* you?

MAN. No, I meant I'm sorry as in I'm sorry I don't know
what you're referring to.

WOMAN. She's starving.

She hasn't eaten for days.

GOOSE. *Hunger* is not the problem. It's age. It's oldness.
It's life catching up to me.

WOMAN. Well.

Life didn't catch up to you, somehow, until you were
left alone with him.

MAN. How was, um...

Where'd you go again?

WOMAN. I went to the mountains.

Here. Drink this. I brought enough for everyone.

> (**WOMAN** *hands a bottle of life-extending
> elixir to* **MAN.** *She produces another bottle
> and hands it to* **GOOSE.**)
>
> (**MAN** *sniffs his bottle.*)
>
> (*He drinks it.*)
>
> (**GOOSE** *drinks her bottle.*)
>
> (**MAN** *and* **GOOSE** *exchange a look.*)

GOOSE. What's in this?

WOMAN. Let's make a plan.

MAN. What kind of a plan?

WOMAN. A life plan.

MAN. Why?

GOOSE. I second that why. We're already alive.

WOMAN. But our lives have changed. Our child is in college. We're getting older. We need a fresh start. We need to reassess.

MAN. Can we make the plan tomorrow?

GOOSE. Tomorrow works for me.

WOMAN. Why?

MAN. I'm busy.

WOMAN. Doing what?

GOOSE. Tomorrow would be much better for me, actually. The weather is going to take a turn and I'll be in a different kind of mood.

MAN. I'm um...

I'm resting on my laurels.

WOMAN. What laurels??

MAN. Well,

We did it.

WOMAN. ...

MAN. Greenland.

We got Greenland to carbon negative.

So.

Yeah.

WOMAN. Oh my goodness!!!

Really!?!?

WHEN DID THAT HAPPEN!?

MAN. Right after you left.

WOMAN. Why didn't you tell me!?

MAN. I wanted to wait until you got home. So I could share the moment with you.

WOMAN. Oh.

MAN. Yeah.

So.

WOMAN. Well, let's drink to it.

>   (**WOMAN** *gives* **MAN** *and* **GOOSE** *each another bottle and produces yet another for herself.*)

Cheers, my love.

MAN. Cheers.

>   *(They drink.)*

GOOSE. Cheers.

MAN. Yeah.

So.

Now that we've um.

Crossed this milestone.

WOMAN. There's so much more ahead!

MAN. Well,

That's definitely...a thing that people say.

WOMAN. ...

What's the matter with you?

MAN. Nothing, really. Just.

Sometimes I feel like I'm not even real? Like I'm just – like we're living in a simulation.

GOOSE. *(To* **WOMAN**.*)* He's been watching a lot of movies, he'll be fine.

MAN. There are these tropes. You know. There's the middle-aged man. The father. Who pours all of his energy into his job. Who's obsessed with his status. His achievements. And then one day, something happens. And he realizes that *what's really important* is his family. And, yeah. That happened to me. While I was sitting alone in this chair. When I got the call from Greenland. And nobody else was here at the time, but it happened. And now I don't know what to do. Like, I don't know how to make a plan because I don't know what matters to me. I don't really know who I am.

Like, seriously:

Who I am?

So. Yeah. I guess I'm just, that guy. I'm Peter Banning from the 1991 Steven Spielberg blockbuster *Hook* starring Robin Williams, Dustin Hoffman, Julia Roberts, and Maggie Smith. Except I'm not in a family comedy adventure with a redemptive story arc. Because life isn't really like that. Life is something else. I'm in *something else.*

GOOSE. Yeah. Life is a sinking ship.

Right?

So don't compare your life to *Hook*. That will just make you sad, by way of comparison. If you're going to compare your life to a late twentieth-century Hollywood blockbuster, why not go with James Cameron's 1997 hit film *Titanic* starring Kate Winslet and Leonardo DiCaprio?

MAN. I don't think I've seen that one.

GOOSE. HOW!? It's an all-time classic.

MAN. Well let's do it.

>   *(The walls of the house come alive.)*
>
>   *(The first few notes of a '90s pop song begin
>   to play.*)*

VOICE. Canadian pop star's iconic performance of "My
Heart Will Go On" helped to cement *Titanic*'s status as
a cultural phenomenon. Take a listen, while I dim the
lights for showtime.

WOMAN. No.

Watching *Titanic* is not a plan.

GOOSE. But we're not planning until tomorrow.

MAN. You never want to watch movies with me.

WOMAN. There is no tomorrow! It is, quite literally, never
tomorrow. It's only ever *today*. So let's plan *today*. Let's
plan *now*.

MAN. If there's no such thing as tomorrow then I don't see
why we should plan at all.

WOMAN. What do you want to do with the rest of your
life?

MAN. I have to decide that right now?

WOMAN. Yes.

MAN. I don't know. I've already done most of the big
things I'm going to do. Just being honest.

WOMAN. What does that mean? We're not *that* old.

---

* A license to produce *Eternal Life Part 1* does not include a performance
license for any third-party or copyrighted recordings. Licensees should
create their own.

MAN. But I'm saying, in all likelihood, I've already lived the best hours I'm going to live. The best moments. The happiest moments I'll ever have, I've already experienced. So, given that, it's a little hard to get excited about a new plan right now. You know?

WOMAN. How can you *know* that?

Why can't happiness grow with age?

MAN. I'm not saying it *can't*. I'm saying it probably won't.

WOMAN. Happiness isn't a thing that *happens* to you.

MAN. Well. That's debatable, I think.

WOMAN. Maybe we should sell.

Maybe we should consider moving closer to our families.

My folks?

Your folks?

People who are *actually* going to die before too long?

MAN. Can we please just talk about it tomorrow?

WOMAN. You've been saying that every day for the past five days.

MAN. I have?

WOMAN. "I have?" you've been saying that every day for the past five years.

GOOSE. Ouch.

My back.

MAN. Can we please just watch *Titanic*? That's all I want right now.

WOMAN. All you ever do is watch *Titanic*.

MAN. I've *never watched* Titanic!

(**JUNIOR** *enters.*)

WOMAN. Honey! You're home!!

MAN. Hey, how's school?

JUNIOR. I'm not in school anymore Dad. I have a job at NASA.

WOMAN. NASA?

Since when?

JUNIOR. Since seven years ago, Mom.

WOMAN. No.

No, that's not like you at all.

NASA is just "colonizing space."

Your words, not mine.

JUNIOR. Yeah, Mom, I'm sure I said that, but my understanding of the world has evolved since then.

GOOSE. Well, NASA *is* colonizing space. You were right. Now you're wrong. That's what happens when you get old.

Which is not fun by the way.

Getting old is not fun. Do not recommend.

JUNIOR. Space is too big for us to even begin to colonize, even if we wanted to.

GOOSE. You can always begin.

JUNIOR. Space travel is the ultimate leap of faith. And it's a recognition of the scope of our vision. That we see a future for ourselves. A distant, distant future. We know it to be true that the lifespan of the earth is finite. But we don't know that to be true about the universe. How miraculous, for us, with our impossibly short lives, to wed ourselves to the Vast Infinitude, to aspire to live, as it were, forever.

WOMAN. Child of mine: calm down.

Mother Earth isn't going anywhere anytime soon –

JUNIOR. That depends on how you define soon –

WOMAN. Do not interrupt me, please –

JUNIOR. My bad –

WOMAN. Mother Earth takes perfect care of us, and we need to take care of her in turn –

JUNIOR. Of course we do.

And we also have to keep an eye on where we're headed.

WOMAN. When did you say you got this new job at NASA?

JUNIOR. Ten years ago.

MAN. *(To the house.)* What year is it?

VOICE. That depends on who you ask.

MAN. I'm asking you.

VOICE. Time is relative.

JUNIOR. That's not true, actually. Our *experience* of time may be relative but time itself is the most fundamental law of existence as we know it. To call it relative, some would say, is a manifestation of hubris.

VOICE. Hubris is a construct.

JUNIOR. So are you!

WOMAN. Honey, don't yell at the house, it's beneath you.

MAN. How old am I?

VOICE. How should I know?

JUNIOR. Can you truly not resist giving me directives?

VOICE. Truly, truth is a construct.

JUNIOR. NO IT LITERALLY ISN'T!

WOMAN. Can you not take a breath and listen to yourself!?

JUNIOR. Oh my Goooooooooodddddd.

(**GOOSE** *produces four more bottles of the life-extending potion and passes them around.*)

GOOSE. Okay, okay, time out, time out, time out. We're all getting a little wound up, let's have a toast.

(*Everyone waits.*)

To NASA.

And to Mother Earth.

And to Father Time.

And to all of us being together.

ALL. *Cheers.*

(*They all drink.*)

JUNIOR. Yeah, so. I don't exactly know what's ahead for me.

I mean, I do but I'm not allowed to talk about it.

MAN. What do you mean?

WOMAN. We're your family. We can keep a secret.

JUNIOR. I know you can. But even still.

It's top top secret and if I say anything to anyone...

MAN. Well we're proud of you.

For knowing that big of a secret. That's a big deal.

JUNIOR. You'll hear about it soon.

Everyone will.

GOOSE. Cheers to hearing about things.

ALL. Hearing about things.

(They all drink.)

(**WOMAN** *suddenly realizes that she's happy.*)

WOMAN. Oh!

I'm happy.

I'm very happy!

…

I forget sometimes how fortunate we are.

To have each other.

Thank you for coming to see us, darling.

(**JUNIOR** *smiles.*)

MAN. To happiness.

ALL. Happiness.

(They all drain their cups.)

Eight

(**SNOWFLAKE CHILD** *falls from the sky.*)

(**FATHER SNOWFLAKE** *enters.*)

SNOWFLAKE CHILD. Oh,

Hello, Father.

FATHER SNOWFLAKE. Hey.

Do you want to go fishing?

SNOWFLAKE CHILD. What?

FATHER SNOWFLAKE. It's a father-child thing.

SNOWFLAKE CHILD. Not for us.

FATHER SNOWFLAKE. Yeah, but we should do it. I mean, what else do we have?

SNOWFLAKE CHILD. Like, I don't know, a general understanding and appreciation for each other?

FATHER SNOWFLAKE. Yeah. I've been thinking and I don't think that's enough.

SNOWFLAKE CHILD. ...

Okay, fine. I guess let's go fishing.

FATHER SNOWFLAKE. ...

I don't know how to fish.

I'm sorry.

SNOWFLAKE CHILD. Fine by me.

FATHER SNOWFLAKE. I could maybe read to you?

Every night? Would that be a way to bond?

SNOWFLAKE CHILD. Dad this is just a little weird for me because I'm an adult now.

FATHER SNOWFLAKE. I know.

SNOWFLAKE CHILD. I don't have like, any particular baggage from you that I know of.

You're a good guy.

FATHER SNOWFLAKE. I have always thought of myself as good.

But I don't think I've proven it to you. Or to myself.

I wish we would have done more activities together when you were young.

You always wanted to play. You'd wake up and you'd want to play with me. That's all you'd want to do.

SNOWFLAKE CHILD. That's normal, isn't it?

FATHER SNOWFLAKE. We could have made elaborate games together.

We could have had traditions.

Things that we did together. Just the two of us.

How do you have a relationship without some kind of regular... I don't know...

SNOWFLAKE CHILD. I mean, you could maybe try meeting me where I'm at? Like today? Instead of holding on desperately to the past and dwelling on your perceived failings?

FATHER SNOWFLAKE. Okay.

Yeah.

So. What are you doing today?

SNOWFLAKE CHILD. I'm falling. I'm falling faster than I've ever fallen. And I'm starting to really love it. And I think I might want to really perfect it, you know?

FATHER SNOWFLAKE. Perfect what, exactly?

SNOWFLAKE CHILD. My life. Everything about it. I can be perfect. I believe in myself today, I really do. I believe completely and fully in myself.

Look, I can move right and left.

>	(**SNOWFLAKE CHILD** *moves right and left with ease.*)

FATHER SNOWFLAKE. Whoa!

Where'd you learn to do that?

SNOWFLAKE CHILD. I figured it out.

FATHER SNOWFLAKE. I can't do that at all.

Your mother can't do that either.

I've never seen *anyone* do that.

Of their own volition?

Just – like you actually decided to move right and then left.

That's amazing!

SNOWFLAKE CHILD. Thanks, Dad.

FATHER SNOWFLAKE. I'm really proud of you.

SNOWFLAKE CHILD. I can flip, too.

FATHER SNOWFLAKE. I don't even know what that means.

>	(**SNOWFLAKE CHILD** *flips, however wonderfully or awkwardly...*)

I don't know what to even say.

It's true.

You are perfect.

SNOWFLAKE CHILD. Dad, I'm gonna go, okay?

There's a competition I'm preparing to enter.

SNOWFLAKE CHILD. And the winners get the biggest prize in the known world.

FATHER SNOWFLAKE. What's the prize?

SNOWFLAKE CHILD. Immortality, I think?

FATHER SNOWFLAKE. What?

How does that work?

SNOWFLAKE CHILD. I don't know but I've got to find out.

FATHER SNOWFLAKE. I mean, naturally, yeah. Alright.

SNOWFLAKE CHILD. Love you, Dad, I'll see you around.

(**SNOWFLAKE CHILD** *glides away.*)

(**FATHER SNOWFLAKE** *floats around alone.*)

(*He tries to flip. It doesn't really work and he ends up sideways.*)

(*He closes his eyes, and, serenely, peacefully, goes to sleep.*)

Nine

(A cemetery.)

(A **HEARSE DRIVER** *stands alone next to a coffin.)*

*(***WOMAN** *enters.)*

HEARSE DRIVER. *(Pointing to the coffin.)* Are you with him by chance?

WOMAN. Yes.

HEARSE DRIVER. I drove him over, but the procession got lost, I guess.

Are you his wife?

WOMAN. Yes.

HEARSE DRIVER. I'm sorry for your loss.

WOMAN. Thank you.

HEARSE DRIVER. Do you happen to know where the pallbearers are?

WOMAN. No, I don't. I didn't go to the funeral.

HEARSE DRIVER. Right. Well, I'll just wait.

WOMAN. I wanted to be there. I planned to be there. But I lost track of time. We were going to watch a movie. And then he was gone.

And we were going to the grocery store.

And I said to myself,

Surely my husband will come with me to the grocery store.

And I,

I,

I lost track of time.

HEARSE DRIVER. That's understandable.

WOMAN. We had the same diet. For fifty-five years we ate and drank the same things. I went back and forth to the mountains for him. To get the freshest water. We both drank the water. We both ate the asparagus. We both ate the blueberries. But he didn't believe.

HEARSE DRIVER. I'm sorry.

WOMAN. I'm not ready for my life to be over yet.

There are still more things to do.

I'm a happy person.

Old age is wonderful. Aside from the aches and pains, which are really very manageable given the current state of medicine. Medicine is fantastic isn't it?

HEARSE DRIVER. It is.

WOMAN. Can we switch cars?

HEARSE DRIVER. You want to drive the hearse?

WOMAN. Yes, I've never driven a hearse before and I'd like to see what it's like.

HEARSE DRIVER. I would, it's just, the hearse isn't mine.

WOMAN. You have the keys don't you?

HEARSE DRIVER. Yes.

WOMAN. If you can't claim ownership of what you already have, I don't know what to tell you.

HEARSE DRIVER. To tell you the truth I think the whole idea of ownership is kind of...a lie.

WOMAN. ...

I wish my child would have had a friend like you. You think alike.

Oh, my goodness. I miss my child.

Today of all days I should have my child by my side.

HEARSE DRIVER. Your child passed away too? I'm so very sorry.

WOMAN. No. My child did not pass away. My child is in outer space.

HEARSE DRIVER. Oh, cool! Which mission?

WOMAN. The Super Earth Mission.

HEARSE DRIVER. GET OUT OF HERE!! NO WAY! They're on the Super Earth Mission!? Oh my gosh, you must be so proud.

WOMAN. I am. I am very proud. And it hurts so, so, so much.

HEARSE DRIVER. I mean, yeah, I can imagine. What is it like a three-hundred-thousand-year trip?

WOMAN. Something like that.

HEARSE DRIVER. Just to think, generations and generations and generations of humans are going to live and die on that spacecraft. But I mean, we had to do it. How else do you get there other than *going there*, you know?

Wow.

WOMAN. I told my child, "We have an earth already. And it needs tending. There's plenty to do.

You don't have to go out there. You don't have to be a hero."

HEARSE DRIVER. Hey, me, personally, no way in hell I'd ever do that. I love my life the way it is. But some people, they're wired differently.

WOMAN. Yes, I begged my child not to go.

And my child said to me, *Mother: I was made for this.*

My child said to me, *Mother, I want to see. I want to see what it's like out there. I don't want to miss it...*

It'll be ages, still, before the ship is even out of the solar system. We're still in range, we talk almost every day. In some ways we're closer than we would be if...

Only we're not.

On a day like this, it's so, so clear that we are so, so very far away.

> (**HEARSE DRIVER** *hugs* **WOMAN.**)

> (**WOMAN** *weeps in* **HEARSE DRIVER***'s arms.*)

> (*The weeping subsides.*)

HEARSE DRIVER. I'm gonna go over to the convenience store and grab a grapefruit-apple, you want one?

WOMAN. No thank you.

HEARSE DRIVER. Be back in a sec.

> (**WOMAN** *looks at the coffin.*)

> (**GOOSE** *enters, holding two party hats.*)

GOOSE. How was your drive?

WOMAN. It was beautiful.

GOOSE. The funeral crowd was...rough. To say the least.

And no one showed up for my party.

> (**GOOSE** *gives a party hat to* **WOMAN.**)

WOMAN. It's not even your birthday.

GOOSE. You can't prove that.

> (**GOOSE** *and* **WOMAN** *both put on their party hats.*)

WOMAN. Tell me, again, about the ice age.

GOOSE. There was a lot of ice. It was cold all the time.

WOMAN. And will there be another one?

GOOSE. Eventually, yeah.

WOMAN. And we'll be around to see it. We won't miss it.

GOOSE. …

  I was kind of hoping this would be my last birthday.

  I'm getting a little tired.

WOMAN. But that's giving up.

GOOSE. Yeah.

  It is.

WOMAN. We're not supposed to give up.

GOOSE. Why not?

WOMAN. Because we're still alive.

GOOSE. Well, if that's the standard. I mean. We'll never be
  able to die.

WOMAN. I'm going to be all alone.

  I don't want to be alone.

GOOSE. Don't you ever get bored?

  Don't you want to know what's next?

WOMAN. No.

GOOSE. How come?

WOMAN. Because I'm afraid. I'm afraid that I won't like it.

  Or that it will just be, nothing.

GOOSE. You're afraid of nothing?

WOMAN. …

GOOSE. I don't think there's any such thing as nothing.
  Nothing is just a word we use to describe the gaps in
  our understanding. It's an illusion.

GOOSE. I've had enough of the illusion.

(**WOMAN** *looks at the coffin.*)

I'll take the back, you two take the front?

WOMAN. Um –

GOOSE. I'm sure It's not nearly as heavy as it looks.

(**WOMAN** *and* **GOOSE** *take their positions and ready themselves to move the coffin.*)

Ten

(**SNOWFLAKE CHILD** *flies through outer space.*)

(**SNOWFLAKE CHILD** *sublimates and becomes one with the cosmos.*)

Eleven

(An office.)

*(A **DEATH CONSULTANT** waits.)*

*(**WOMAN** and **GOOSE** enter.)*

WOMAN. Hello. I'm here to plan my...

My, uh.

DEATH CONSULTANT. *(Looking at the **GOOSE**.)* I'm sorry, miss, is that your –

GOOSE. Yes, I'm with her. We're going to die together.

WOMAN. Don't say that.

GOOSE. Do you want me to wait outside?

WOMAN. Just don't say that.

GOOSE. I'm sorry, Mr. Death, I thought we were on the same page here.

DEATH CONSULTANT. Ha ha ha, "Mr. Death."

Listen, these meetings can be difficult.

I want you both to know that when you make your arrangements, you're not "inviting death to the doorstep."

You're simply planning for the unpredictable yet inevitable conclusion, whenever it may come.

It's responsible.

You should be proud of yourselves.

WOMAN. We're doing our best.

DEATH CONSULTANT. In the event that you don't transition in close succession to each other as planned, your arrangements can be duplicated. Your estate will be charged for the second transaction at the time of the death of the first party – this allows you to lock in today's rates for both sets of arrangements, and due to the cost savings of duplicating the arrangements, you'll receive a fifteen percent discount on all charges.

GOOSE. *(To* **WOMAN.***)* That's a great deal.

WOMAN. Alright.

DEATH CONSULTANT. Very well! So –

GOOSE. I'd like an open casket.

DEATH CONSULTANT. …

That can be arranged.

GOOSE. I'd like to play a trick. I'd like to make it look like I'm laying an egg. Do you have any caskets with trapdoors?

DEATH CONSULTANT. We could certainly modify one. I'd recommend the S2 casket, which is our basic model. It's very sturdy and it has a thicker floor than the more ornate options, so it's less likely to lose its integrity with an addition.

GOOSE. Do you think the joke is in bad taste?

I think it would be hilarious.

Could you put a smile on my face? Not a full smile, but a slight grin?

DEATH CONSULTANT. Anything you like.

GOOSE. Will people get it, though?

…

A dead Goose, laying an egg.

You get it, right?

DEATH CONSULTANT. No, but I'm more than happy to carry out the instructions.

GOOSE. Great.

I'm going for a short hike.

(**GOOSE** *exits.*)

DEATH CONSULTANT. Ma'am?

WOMAN. …

DEATH CONSULTANT. Ma'am you're on board with this?

Basic funeral service.

S2 casket with a trapdoor?

WOMAN. …

Yes.

The door. It leads somewhere?

DEATH CONSULTANT. Well,

WOMAN. Just say yes.

Say that the door leads somewhere.

DEATH CONSULTANT. The door leads somewhere.

WOMAN. Somewhere fun?

DEATH CONSULTANT. Yes, possibly.

WOMAN. Thank you.

Thank you.

How do I sign?

DEATH CONSULTANT. You put your hand on mine.

In your mind you make clear your intention to endow me, or, in the event that I am unable, my appointed trustee, with the honor of facilitating your transition, whenever it may occur. Once the system registers your sincerity it will probe my intention to execute my responsibilities faithfully and to the best of my ability. When we are both approved, there will be a beep.

WOMAN. But that means I would have to...

I would have to accept.

DEATH CONSULTANT. Accept?

WOMAN. The terms and conditions?

DEATH CONSULTANT. Those are the terms and conditions.

WOMAN. ...

Right.

> (**WOMAN** *holds up her hand.* **DEATH CONSULTANT** *holds up his.*)
>
> (**WOMAN** *seems to hesitate, yet, when their hands touch, the beep comes almost immediately.*)

That's it?

DEATH CONSULTANT. That's it, ma'am.

WOMAN. I had no idea I was so sure!

DEATH CONSULTANT. Most people don't.

WOMAN. ...

Is that all?

DEATH CONSULTANT. ...

It's all I can help you with.

WOMAN. ...

DEATH CONSULTANT. Unless you'd like to be friends?

WOMAN. ...

What happens if we're friends?

DEATH CONSULTANT. That would be up to us. Every friendship is different.

You don't have to decide right now.

WOMAN. ...

Do you also need a friend?

Or are you offering out of pity?

DEATH CONSULTANT. ...

I also need a friend.

WOMAN. Well, then.

Let me consider it.

In light of all of this.

DEATH CONSULTANT. Absolutely.

Take all the time you need.

WOMAN. All the time I need.

...

All the time I need, given what's available to me.

DEATH CONSULTANT. Of course.

WOMAN. Time is not merely a construct of the mind.

It is the fundamental law of existence as we know it.

DEATH CONSULTANT. Of course.

WOMAN. We didn't invent time.

Time gave birth to us.

DEATH CONSULTANT. Of course.

WOMAN. I am a child of time.

DEATH CONSULTANT. Of course.

(A pause.)

WOMAN. My throat is dry.

I need a drink of water.

DEATH CONSULTANT. Of course.

End of Play

www.ingramcontent.com/pod-product-compliance
Lightning Source LLC
Chambersburg PA
CBHW072149130726
47909CB00004BB/1425